D0893893

The European Union

Political, Social, and Economic Cooperation

THE
EUROPEAN UNION

POLITICAL, SOCIAL, AND ECONOMIC COOPERATION

FINLAND

by
Nicole Sia

Mason Crest Publishers
Philadelphia

Mason Crest Publishers Inc.
370 Reed Road, Broomall, Pennsylvania 19008
(866) MCP-BOOK (toll free)
www.masoncrest.com

First printing
1 2 3 4 5 6 7 8 9 10

Library of Congress Cataloging-in-Publication Data

Sia, Nicole.
  Finland / by Nicole Sia.
       p. cm.—(European Union)
  Includes index.
    ISBN 1-4222-0046-9
    ISBN 1-4222-0038-8 (series)
  1. Finland—Juvenile literature. 2. European Union—Finland—Juvenile literature. I. Title. II. European Union (Series) (Philadelphia, Pa.)
  DL1012.S53 2006
  948.97—dc22
                          2005016555

Produced by Harding House Publishing Service, Inc.
www.hardinghousepages.com
Interior design by Benjamin Stewart.
Cover design by MK Bassett-Harvey.
Printed in the Hashemite Kingdom of Jordan.

CONTENTS

THE
EUROPEAN
UNION

ICELAND

GREENLAND SEA

BARENTS SEA

NORWEGIAN SEA

WHITE SEA

RUSSIA

FINLAND

Gulf of Bothnia

Helsinki

NORWAY

Oslo

SWEDEN

Stockholm

ESTONIA

Tallinn

Gulf of Finland

Tartu

Gulf of Riga

LATVIA

Riga

Moscow

DENMARK

Aalborg

BALTIC SEA

LITHUANIA

Klaipeda

Kaunas

Vilnius

RUSSIA

Minsk

UNITED KINGDOM

Edinburgh

Belfast

NORTH SEA

Copenhagen

Malmö

BELARUS

IRELAND

Dublin

Irish Sea

Liverpool

Manchester

Hamburg

Gdańsk

POLAND

Warsaw

Kraków

Kyiv

THE NETHERLANDS

The Hague

Rotterdam Amsterdam

Berlin

Leipzig

Wrocław

St. George's Channel

Birmingham

London

English Channel

Düsseldorf

Cologne

GERMANY

Dresden

UKRAINE

BELGIUM

Brussels

LUXEMBOURG

Luxembourg

Frankfurt Main

Plzeň

Prague

CZECH REPUBLIC

Brno

Košice

SLOVAKIA

Paris

Stuttgart

Munich

Vienna

Bratislava

Budapest

MOLDOVA

Chișinău

Sea of Azov

Nantes

FRANCE

Basel

Bern

SWITZERLAND

Zürich

Salzburg

AUSTRIA

Graz

HUNGARY

Szeged

ROMANIA

Bucharest

Bay of Biscay

Bordeaux

Lyons

Geneva

Milan

Ljubljana

Trieste

Zagreb

SLOVENIA

Belgrade

BLACK SEA

Turin

Venice

BOSNIA-HERCEGOVINA

CROATIA

YUGOSLAVIA

Sofia

BULGARIA

Toulouse

Marseille

Nice

ADRIATIC SEA

Vigo

Bilbao

Florence

Gulf of Lion

Barcelona

ITALY

Rome

MACEDONIA

Skopje

Ankara

TURKEY

PORTUGAL

Porto

Lisbon

Madrid

TYRRHENIAN SEA

Naples

ALBANIA

Thessaloniki

AEGEAN SEA

SPAIN

Valencia

Seville

Faro

Strait of Gibraltar

IONIAN SEA

GREECE

Athens

Kalamata

Sea of Crete

Lefkosia (Nicosia)

CYPRUS

SYR

MEDITERRANEAN SEA

Algiers

Tunis

MALTA

Valetta

LEBANON

Damascus

JOR

Rabat

MOROCCO

ALGERIA

TUNISIA

MEDITERRANEAN SEA

Tripoli

ISRAEL & THE PALESTINIAN TERRITORIES

Amman

LIBYA

EGYPT

Cairo

FINLAND

European Union Member since 1995

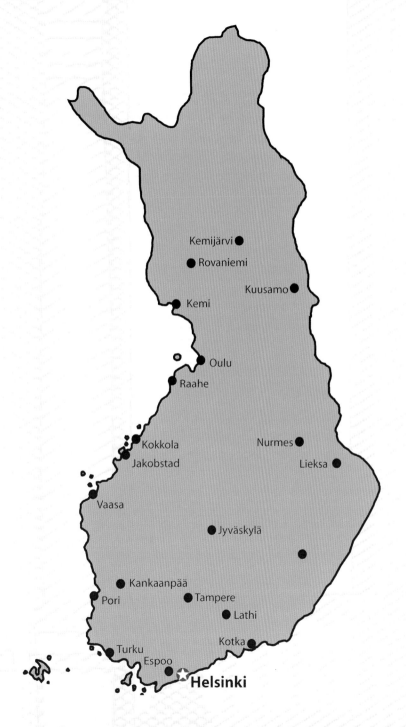

Kemijärvi

Rovaniemi

Kuusamo

Kemi

Oulu

Raahe

Kokkola

Jakobstad

Nurmes

Lieksa

Vaasa

Jyväskylä

Kankaanpää

Pori

Tampere

Lathi

Turku

Kotka

Espoo

Helsinki

INTRODUCTION

Sixty years ago, Europe lay scarred from the battles of the Second World War. During the next several years, a plan began to take shape that would unite the countries of the European continent so that future wars would be inconceivable. On May 9, 1950, French Foreign Minister Robert Schuman issued a declaration calling on France, Germany, and other European countries to pool together their coal and steel production as "the first concrete foundation of a European federation." "Europe Day" is celebrated each year on May 9 to commemorate the beginning of the European Union (EU).

The EU consists of twenty-five countries, spanning the continent from Ireland in the west to the border of Russia in the east. Eight of the ten most recently admitted EU member states are former communist regimes that were behind the Iron Curtain for most of the latter half of the twentieth century.

Any European country with a democratic government, a functioning market economy, respect for fundamental rights, and a government capable of implementing EU laws and policies may apply for membership. Bulgaria and Romania are set to join the EU in 2007. Croatia and Turkey have also embarked on the road to EU membership.

While the EU began as an idea to ensure peace in Europe through interconnected economies, it has evolved into so much more today:

- Citizens can travel freely throughout most of the EU without carrying a passport and without stopping for border checks.

- EU citizens can live, work, study, and retire in another EU country if they wish.

- The euro, the single currency accepted throughout twelve of the EU countries (with more to come), is one of the EU's most tangible achievements, facilitating commerce and making possible a single financial market that benefits both individuals and businesses.

- The EU ensures cooperation in the fight against cross-border crime and terrorism.

- The EU is spearheading world efforts to preserve the environment.

- As the world's largest trading bloc, the EU uses its influence to promote fair rules for world trade, ensuring that globalization also benefits the poorest countries.

- The EU is already the world's largest donor of humanitarian aid and development assistance, providing 55 percent of global official development assistance to developing countries in 2004.

The EU is neither a nation intended to replace existing nations, nor an international organization. The EU is unique—its member countries have established common institutions to which they delegate some of their sovereignty so that decisions on matters of joint interest can be made democratically at the European level.

Europe is a continent with many different traditions and languages, but with shared values such as democracy, freedom, and social justice, cherished values well known to North Americans. Indeed, the EU motto is "United in Diversity."

Enjoy your reading. Take advantage of this chance to learn more about Europe and the EU!

Ambassador John Bruton,
Head of Delegation of the European Commission, Washington, D.C.

One of Finland's many lakes.

CHAPTER 1 THE LANDSCAPE

Welcome to Finland, a country of undulating hills, peaceful marshlands, forested islands, and countless lakes. From the arctic weathers of the rugged far north, to the temperate climate of its heavily populated south, Finland boasts a culture rich with tradition and a landscape full of beauty. The land as we know it today was molded long ago when continental glaciers etched shapes into the surface of

GEOGRAPHY

Thousands of years ago, glaciers moved over the land, carving out thousands of lakes. As the glaciers melted, the lakes filled with their water. Moraines—piles of boulders, rocks, and other debris—were carried and deposited as the melting glaciers moved. Drumlins, long hills or ridges resulting from glacial movement, and eskers, long ridges of gravel, accumulated as a stream flowed beneath a melting glacier.

The glaciers pushed down much of the land, and today, through a process known as isostatic rebound, the country continues to slowly lift from the sea. As this occurs, Finland's total land mass grows about 2.7 square miles (7 sq. kilometers) a year. Currently, Finland is 130,559 square miles (338,145 sq. kilometers), just slightly smaller than Montana.

To the north, Finland borders Norway; to the west, Sweden; and then it extends east into Russia, where no natural border separates the two countries. The country's coastline is **perforated** by many bays and inlets, and touches the Gulf of Finland (to the south), the Baltic Sea (to the southwest), and the Gulf of Bothnia (to the west). Finland is made up of four geographic regions that all share similar physical characteristics.

Archipelago Finland is composed of thousands of tiny islands located in and around the southwestern coast and into the Baltic Sea. As land depressed from glacial activity continues to rise to the surface, more islands will form. Many of the islands are covered with forests and bare bedrock. Most significant of these islands are the Åland Islands. During the winter, frozen seawaters link the islands to the mainland, forming a strategic barrier important to the country's defense.

About a third of upland Finland is found in the **Arctic Circle** and then extends farther into the far-northern region known as Lapland, or Saamiland. Unlike the smooth, rolling hills of the south, the upland's northern hills are rugged. Because of its location, the region is covered in **arctic scrub**, though, like much of the southern landscape, there are areas of soft, naturally waterlogged ground called bogs.

Finland's interior lake district makes up the largest portion of the landscape. This centrally located **plateau** region is characterized by some 60,000 shallow lakes and hilly, forested countryside. The largest of these lakes is Lake Saimaa, the fifth-largest lake in Europe.

Coastal Finland, because of its broad clay plains, is used primarily for agriculture and dairy farming. This area slopes south from the Salpausselka Ridges, and southwest from the upland areas. It runs into the central plateau of the interior lake district.

CLIMATE

Finland is warmer than other countries found at the same latitude (between the sixtieth and seventieth northern parallels). The **proximity** of the Baltic Sea, the country's many interior waters, and warmed winds blowing off the Atlantic Ocean raise Finland's average temperature. Summers are short but warm, usually beginning in late May and lasting until mid-September. Sometimes weather drifts over the Eurasian continent, bringing extreme heat in summer and severe cold in winter. Winter months are typically cold and wet, lasting about three months on the archipelago and five to seven months in Lapland.

Rainfall is moderate during all seasons, but the north's long winters cause half the annual precipitation—about eighteen inches (460 millimeters) in

Finland's long, cold winter

The countryside around Helsinki

the north and twenty-eight inches (710 millimeters) in the south—to fall as snow. Areas of Finland located in the Arctic Circle experience polar days, periods of twenty-four-hour sunlight. These periods can last for about two and a half months. During the winter, stargazers may catch a glimpse of the dancing Aurora Borealis, the northern lights.

WILDLIFE

Finland is a temperate **coniferous-mixed** forest zone. Its forests cover more than two-thirds of the land, making it the most densely forested country in Europe. Lush woods provide habitats for thousands of species of plants and animals. Aspen, alder, maple, and elm trees are found in the far south; spruce and pine grow in Finland's northern forests. In the less-populated northern regions, bear, wolf, lynx, and arctic fox can be found, as well as birds like wild geese, swans, snow bunting, and golden plovers. Reindeer also inhabit Finland, but their population is thinning.

About 10 percent of Finland is covered by water, which includes both fresh and saltwater bodies. Perch, salmon, trout, and pike can be found in freshwater lakes. Cod, herring, and haddock are fished in the salty oceans.

Six percent of the total land is designated for parks and other wildlife reserves, and the country maintains a remarkably low deforestation rate. Finland boasts air quality superior to other European nations, but ecological problems such as air pollution and acid rain continue to result from the south's dense industrial and urban populations.

QUICK FACTS: THE GEOGRAPHY OF FINLAND

Location: Northern Europe, bordering the Baltic Sea, Gulf of Bothnia, and Gulf of Finland, between Sweden and Russia

Area: (slightly smaller than Montana)
total: 130,559 square miles (338,145 sq. km.)
land: 117,558 square miles (304,473 sq. km.)
water: 13,001 square miles (33,672 sq. km.)

Borders: Norway 457 miles (736 km.); Sweden 382 miles (614 km.); Russia 833 miles (1,340 km.)

Climate: cold temperate; potentially subarctic but comparatively mild because of the effects of the North Atlantic Current, Baltic Sea, and more than 60,000 lakes

Terrain: mostly low, flat to rolling plains with scattered lakes and low hills

Elevation extremes:
lowest point: Baltic Sea—0 feet (0 meters)
highest point: Halti—4,357 feet (1,328 meters)

Natural hazards: none

Source: www.cia.org, 2005.

The Presidential Palace in Helsinki.

2 FINLAND'S HISTORY AND GOVERNMENT

In the 1990s, archaeologists discovered evidence showing that human settlement in Finland might date back more than 100,000 years. Until these findings, historians believed the area did not become inhabited until around

8000 BCE by **Neolithic** peoples, hunter-gatherer tribes that migrated from the east. Still, little is known about these earliest settlements. Around 3000 BCE, a pottery-making culture, the Comb-Ceramic, occupied the area. Indo-Europeans may have introduced agriculture and navigation skills to Finland between 1800 and 1600 BCE, and eventually **assimilated** into the indigenous population. This combination of tribes formed the Kiukainen culture (1600–1200 BCE).

FINNS OR FENNI?

The Roman historian Tacitus made the first recorded reference to the Finns in 98 CE. Tacitus describes the "Fenni," who are now believed to be the Saamis—a tribe who spoke a Finno-Urgic language (one similar to Finnish), but who resisted assimilation with the Finns.

During Finland's Iron Age, other tribes, such as the Suomalaiset of the southwest, the Karelians of the east, and the Estonians of the south, expanded throughout Finland's countryside. They also merged with the people already settled there. The tribes would be threatened by more politically and technologically advanced Viking cultures.

THE VIKINGS

Between the sixth and eleventh centuries CE, Swedish Vikings used the Aland Islands as a central point from which to **pillage** and trade with Russia. Although they built no permanent settlements in Finland, the Finns benefited from trading colonies built by Swedish merchants. This helped the Finnic tribes expand farther in each direction. However, the Finns did not yet establish a unified government.

SWEDISH RULE

When Christianity swept most of Europe, Finland became a sitting duck for both Sweden and Russia, who sought to both convert its inhabitants and exploit its economic possibilities. The Roman Catholic Swedes began missionary activities in the west during the twelfth-century **Crusades**, while the Russians converted eastern Finnic peoples like the Karelians to the Eastern Orthodox Church. Late. in the thirteenth century, Sweden made a final attempt to secure Finland as its own, but what resulted was thirty years of war. In 1323, the Peace of Pahkinasaari established a border between Finland and Russia, ending the conflict. With this new development, Sweden was able to gradually take control of all of Finland.

MEDIEVAL FINLAND

As the Swedes integrated Finland into its political structure, the Finns were left with little say in politics or the economy. Hunting, fishing, trapping, and gathering now replaced farming as the primary method of earning a living. The country was divided into social classes: clergy were ranked first, followed by the Swedish-speaking nobility; the

burghers were the middle class; and then at the bottom of the social structure were the farmers. Finland was represented in the Swedish **Diet** of the Four Estates and maintained some control over local government. The importance of the Roman Catholic Church grew as it was used as a place for local government and education.

MARTIN LUTHER AND THE REFORMATION

In 1517, Martin Luther, a German monk, nailed his ninety-five **theses** to a church door in Germany. The document challenged the Roman Catholic Church to give up its interest in worldly affairs like politics, power, and wealth, which Luther judged to be corruptive forces. The theses also called for an end to the **hierarchal** order of worship. Luther believed that each individual believer has a personal relationship with God. Followers of Luther became known as Protestants.

Lutheranism swept through Germany and was adopted in Sweden-Finland in 1598 when Sigismund, the last Catholic king, was overthrown. Because the Reformation focused so heavily on religious instruction, its spread encouraged a rise in literacy; in 1640, it led to the founding of Abo Academy, a school that trained Finnish clergy.

THE GREAT WRATH AND THE AGE OF FREEDOM

At the very beginning of the eighteenth century, Denmark, Poland, and Russia formed an alliance in an effort to break up Sweden's control over most of the Baltic area. In the ensuing conflicts, Finnish soldiers were drafted to fight for the Swedes. Meanwhile, a terrible famine crippled the nation, killing about one-third of Finland's population. Russian troops ravaged the countryside in an attempt to disrupt Swedish commerce. By 1721, Russia had replaced Sweden's control over the Baltic area and was **ceded** some land along

DATING SYSTEMS AND THEIR MEANING

You might be accustomed to seeing dates expressed with the abbreviations BC or AD, as in the year 1000 BC or the year AD 1900. For centuries, this dating system has been the most common in the Western world. However, since BC and AD are based on Christianity (BC stands for Before Christ and AD stands for *anno Domini*, Latin for "in the year of our Lord"), many people now prefer to use abbreviations that people from all religions can be comfortable using. The abbreviations BCE (meaning Before Common Era) and CE (meaning Common Era) mark time in the same way (for example, 1000 BC is the same year as 1000 BCE, and AD 1900 is the same year as 1900 CE), but BCE and CE do not have the same religious overtones as BC and AD.

Finland's southeastern border. Today, the Finns regard this time as the Great Wrath.

After Sweden's defeat, King Charles XII institut-

ERIK IX AND HENRY

As legend goes, the Swedish king Erik IX and the English monk Henry, with encouragement from the pope, led a crusade to convert the polytheistic Finns to Christianity and establish economic and political control. Erik and Henry were successful, but for only a short time. Henry was martyred in Finland and today is revered as the country's patron saint.

ed several political policies that gave more importance to Sweden's **parliament** than to its monarchy. These policies led to conflict between Sweden's two political parties, the Hats—the upper classes—and the Caps—the lower classes. In 1741, the Hats attacked Russia to regain what Sweden had lost in the previous war. Russia again occupied Finland, during what is now called the Lesser Wrath, but at the battle's end, Finland was left owning a larger portion of its land.

THE END OF SWEDISH RULE

The French emperor Napoleon Bonaparte quickly rose to power in France during the late eighteenth century. With a lust to control Europe, Bonaparte cleverly formed an alliance with Russia in 1807 and urged its ruler, Tsar Alexander I, to invade Finland. By 1809, Finland was completely conquered. On September 17, Sweden formally ceded control of Finland to Russia in the Treaty of Hamina.

Under new Russian rule, Finland was granted status as a Grand Duchy—an **autonomous** state. Its laws were left intact, and Alexander restored the lands Finland had lost during the eighteenth century. The Government Council was formed as the premier legislative body in the Grand Duchy. Finland's **customs system** was also preserved; Finnish soldiers were not required to fight in Russian wars; and money collected in taxes did not go outside the country. The tsar did retain **autocratic** rule, however, and could convene the Senate to introduce new legislation without acknowledgment from the Finnish Diet. This period of Finland's history under Russian rule was a peaceful time of growth, free of war and harsh circumstance.

THE RISE OF NATIONALISM AND THE CALL FOR INDEPENDENCE

The 1700s were marked by Finnish resentment of Swedish rule. This was due in part to the fact that the Swedes had forced their language into government and education. In the nine-

teenth century, a wave of **nationalism** swept across Finland, and Finnish became more popularly used; in 1892 it became the country's second official language. In 1835, *The Kalevala*, the first national **epic**, was published. It chronicled the myths, legends, and the folklore of the Karelian people and helped bolster a Finnish sense of national pride.

Another factor feeding Finnish nationalism was **Russification**. Although Finland enjoyed more autonomy as a Grand Duchy, new oppressions came hand-in-hand with Russian rule. The combina-

The Swedish language University in Turku is a reminder of Finland's historical connections to Sweden.

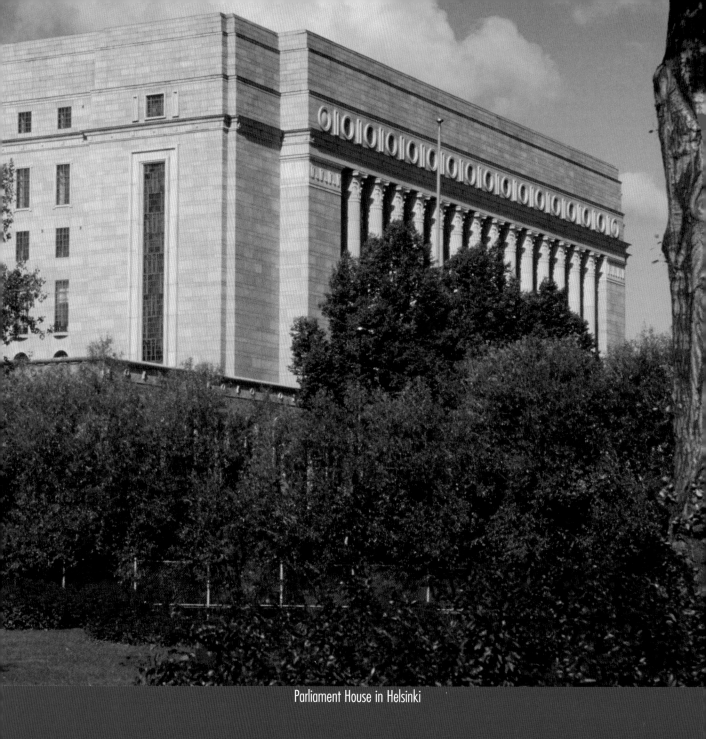
Parliament House in Helsinki

tion of both heightened nationalism and resistance to Russification led Finns to push for their independence. Fortunately for Finland, internal conflict in Russia would present a perfect opportunity for the province to break free.

A slew of Russian civil wars beginning in 1905 allowed Finland to accomplish two important achievements. First, Finland replaced its **antiquated** government institutions with a **unicameral** parliament called the *Eduskunta*. This new government was elected through **universal suffrage**—women were granted the vote; Finland was the first nation in Europe to give women this right. Second, by 1917, during another Russian revolution, Finland managed to break away completely from the empire, declaring independence on December 6. What immediately followed was a year of domestic conflict among Finns, marked by vast political differences. With the help of German forces, **right-wing** Finns were able to take control of the country, **estranging** many citizens from those in power.

A Fledgling Nation

A new Finnish constitution was drafted by mid-1919; it outlined a modern parliamentary system of government, keeping intact the *Edskunta* while creating a presidency, **cabinet**, and independent judiciary. These three branches of government were given overlapping powers that functioned as a system of **checks and balances**.

In the following years, several European nations struggled with communism and **fascist** leaders, but Finland was exposed only briefly to these problems. Communist groups were banned in Finland, so party members joined with the *Maalaisliitto* (ML)—the Agrarian Party—forming the Red-Earth coalition. This new group would remain the most common party for the next fifty years.

Before World War II, Finland's economy flourished with the help of government intervention. Plots of land were redistributed among landless workers, rejuvenating Finnish agriculture. Forestry remained an important source of income, but paper and pulp products replaced timber as the primary export.

The War Years

Finland's official policy of neutrality was not enough to keep it uninvolved in World War II. Because of its uninhibited eastern border with the Soviet Union, German forces **coveted** control of the passageway to lead an attack, while Soviets clamored to occupy it to defend against such an attack. When Finland refused to cede the territory along the border to the Soviets, the Soviets led an attack to take the land in a conflict called the Winter War. The war ended in March 1940, with Finland defeated and agreeing to allot 10 percent of its territory for Soviet military bases. The following year, Finland joined Germany in attacking the Soviet Union. This alliance caused Great Britain to declare war on Finland. Finland won some early battles, but the small nation could not put down the powerful **Allies**. Then in 1944, Finland was forced to sign an **armistice** with the Soviet Union. In it the country surrendered more land, agreed to pay steep **reparations**, and removed German forces from its territory. In the Treaty of Paris of 1947, the capacity of Finland's military was substantially restricted; weapons could only be used in defense. Still, at the war's end, Finland had managed to remain an unoccupied and independent nation.

The following year, the Treaty of Friendship, Cooperation, and Mutual Assistance was drafted with the Soviet Union. The treaty prescribed that under threat of attack, Finland would side with the Soviets in order to keep the border between the two countries secure. This gave the Soviets the defense they desired and ensured that Finland would not have to fear a **preemptive** seizure of territory along its eastern border.

By 1952, Finland had completed paying reparations to the Soviets, and in 1956, the USSR restored control of the territories taken during wartime to the Finns.

JOINING THE COMMUNITY OF NATIONS

Since the years following the war, Finland has become involved with several world organizations. In 1955, it joined the United Nations (UN), and the Nordic Council; in 1961, it joined the European Free Trade Association (EFTA) as an associate, and in 1986, became a full member; in 1989, it joined the Council of Europe; and in 1995, it became a member of the European Union (EU). Finland has been especially active in world peacekeeping measures through the UN, its support of the Nordic Nuclear-Weapons-Free Zone, and its participation in the Helsinki Accords of 1975, which outlined methods of security and cooperation between European countries.

THE ERA OF CONSENSUS, 1966–1981

Finnish politics became decreasingly **adversarial** during the "Era of Consensus." Politics centered on domestic issues, specifically on how to balance Finland's struggling northern and eastern agricultural regions with the spread of **urbanization** in the south and west, and how to reduce the country's reliance on export goods. This common goal encouraged various political parties to work cooperatively, since members of all parties were invested in Finland's economic future; the Social Democratic Party (SDP) aligned with the communist-affiliated ML (which later renamed itself the Center Party). The Red-Earth coalition participated in government for the first time in several years. Two competing labor unions also combined during this spirit of consensus, creating the Central

The Senate building in Helsinki

Organization of the Finnish Trade Unions in 1969, which grew to represent over 85 percent of Finland's total workforce.

The Era of Consensus was a very stable time in Finnish politics. Along with political consensus, social consensus grew as well. Cultural differences between Finnish- and Swedish-speaking Finns declined as **Finnicization** spread, and some of the Swedish-speaking population immigrated to Sweden. Social differences between the working and middle classes also declined.

Helsinki's old government buildings

FINLAND'S MODERN GOVERNMENT

Today the **Republic** of Finland has three branches of government: the executive, legislative, and judicial. The executive branch consists of the president, who is elected by **popular vote** for a six-year term; the prime minister and the deputy prime minister, who are both appointed by the president following approval from parliament; and the Council of State, or the cabinet, which is also appointed by the president pending parliamentary endorsement.

The legislative branch consists of the Eduskunta, which holds 200 members elected by popular vote. In March of 2000, a new constitution came into effect, increasing the parliamentary features of Finnish government.

The judicial branch consists of the *Korkein Oikeus*, or the Supreme Court. The president appoints judges. Popular political parties include the Center Party, or the Kesks; the SDP; the National Coalition Party, or the Kok; the Left Alliance, or VAS, which is a combination of the People's Democratic League and the Democratic Alternative; the Green League, or VIHR; and the Christian Democrats, or the KD.

Market square in Turku, Finland

3 THE ECONOMY

Today, Finland is a highly industrialized nation that is at the forefront in the production of wireless technologies. It operates as a free-market economy, and its *per capita* output matches roughly that of the United Kingdom, France,

Germany, and Italy. Engineering and metal industries lead the economy, while wood and paper industries—Finland's more traditional exports—have taken a backseat in the past thirty years. Paper makes up a third of Finland's principal exports, alongside electronics and machinery.

GADGET COUNTRY

According to the World Economic Forum, Finland ranks first as the world's most competitive country, making the United States second. This is due primarily to the tremendous growth experienced in Finland's electronics and telecommunications sectors in the 1990s. Nokia, a world leader in mobile communications and cell phone technologies, is perhaps the most recognizable Finnish company. Other important products that have originated in Finland include the computer operating system Linux, Polar Electro heart-rate monitors, and Swan Luxury sailboats.

Trade is important; the climate prevents agriculture from producing more than what keeps Finland self-sufficient, leaving none for export. The country must also import oil and other sources of energy, and raw materials for manufacturing.

Exports make up two-fifths of Finland's **gross domestic product (GDP)**. Machinery, engineering, and electronics are primary export markets. The nation's most abundant and valuable natural resource, forests, accounts for one-third of all exports. Spruce, pine, and silver birch trees are the

QUICK FACTS: THE ECONOMY OF FINLAND

Gross Domestic Product (GDP): US$151.2 billion

GDP per capita: US$29,000

Industries: metal products, electronics, shipbuilding, pulp and paper, copper refining, foodstuffs, chemicals, textiles, clothing

Agriculture: barley, wheat, sugar beets, potatoes; dairy cattle; fish

Export commodities: machinery and equipment, chemicals, metals; timber, paper, pulp (1999)

Export partners: Germany 11.8%, Sweden 9.9%, U.S. 8.2%, UK 8%, Russia 7.5%, Netherlands 4.8% (2003)

Import commodities: foodstuffs, petroleum and petroleum products, chemicals, transport equipment, iron and steel, machinery, textile yarn and fabrics, grains (1999)

Import partners: Germany 16.3%, Sweden 14.2%, Russia 11.6%, Netherlands 6.3%, Denmark 5.8%, UK 5.3%, France 4.4% (2003)

Currency: euro

Currency exchange rate: US$1 = .81€ (June 6, 2005)

Note: All figures are 2004 estimates unless noted.
Source: www.cia.org, 2005.

most heavily exported species.

Finland has rich deposits of metallic ores from which copper, zinc, iron, and nickel are made. Lead, vanadium, silver, and gold are mined commercially. Forestry provides job opportunities in rural areas. Still, despite Finland's economic successes, the country suffers from high unemployment rates.

An Economy with Agricultural Roots

Historically, Finland was known for its farming and forest economy. Evidence of agricultural settlement dates back to 1800 BCE. During the *medieval* ages, the Finns expanded north into the forests, cleared the land, and established agricultural communities. Peasants made a living predominantly through farming, but a short growing season led many to hunting and fishing as supplementary means of income. Lumber began to emerge as an important export in the late 1800s, but by the turn of the twentieth century, farmers still made up 70 percent of Finland's workforce.

In response to Russian demand for supplies during World War I, Finland's metalworking and shipbuilding businesses grew rapidly, but Russia's Bolshevik Revolution of 1917 made trade impossible. Like most nations during the *Great Depression*, Finland struggled economically and relied on aid from the United States to avoid starvation. Trade with other western European nations opened, however, and the nation was able to gain much needed imports to supplement its food supply. Paper production, Finland's largest industry, actually grew during the Depression years. But these gains would be undone by German occupation in World War II.

Finland's exhausted economy could not immediately rebound after World War II. Reparations absorbed half the nation's output, and high rates of inflation upset workers, which in turn threatened production rates. But in the 1950s, the Korean War made Finland the uncontested provider of metal goods to the Soviet Union. At the same time, Sweden and the United States began to invest in Finnish markets, which financed expansions in *infrastructure*, agriculture, and industry. Finland's industry continued to grow and prosper through the 1980s, and finally into the explosive telecommunications boom of the 1990s, which allowed the nation to emerge as a highly competitive developer of Internet and wireless technologies.

The Current Currency

Because Finland's rule has changed hands so many times, the nation has used several forms of currency over the years. In fact, the Finnish word for money, *raha*, is derived from the word for "fur," pointing to the prevalence of fur trading in prehistoric ages.

Under Swedish rule, Finland was forced to adopt Swedish currency, including the large, silver coin *taler*, or in the United States, the dollar; *ore*; *marks*; and the *riksdaler*, which was divided into forty-eight *skillings*.

In 1809, Finland was surrendered to Russia, at which time the *ruble*, created both in paper and silver, became the primary monetary unit. Other Russian-issued currency included the *kopek*, a smaller denomination. In 1860, Finland was granted a currency of its own, the *markka*, which was divided into 100 *penni*. The markka was valued at one-fourth the ruble.

Since 1999, Finland has adopted the euro as its primary currency, and as of January 1, 2002, the markka and penni have been withdrawn from

Finland's farmland

circulation, replaced by euro denominations. In Finland, the national side of a coined euro depicts the same heraldic lion that was originally printed on Finnish coins of the 1860s.

TRANSPORTATION

The state maintains Finland's roads and railways. National highways that span the country were mostly complete by the mid-1980s, while local roads continued to be established. The railways were slow to develop; the country continued to lay tracks until the early 1970s. The lumber industry uses Finland's system of canals for an efficient way of transporting raw materials. The canals connect interior lakes to one another and to the Gulf of Finland. Finnair, the national airline, carries both domestic and international flights. Major airports are located in Helsinki, Turku, Rovaniemi, Oulu, and Tampere.

ALEKSIS KIVI

The Finnish National Theatre in Helsinki

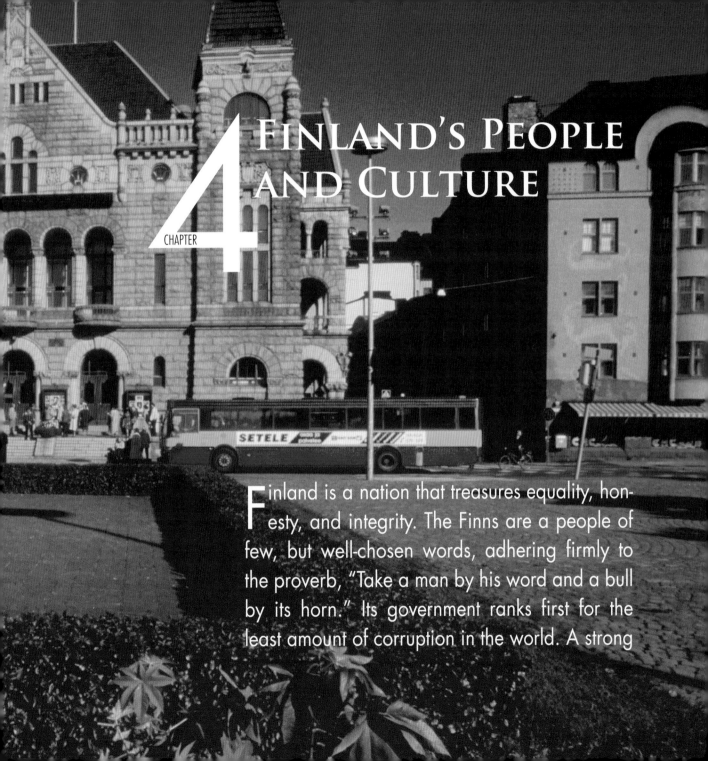

FINLAND'S PEOPLE AND CULTURE

CHAPTER **4**

Finland is a nation that treasures equality, honesty, and integrity. The Finns are a people of few, but well-chosen words, adhering firmly to the proverb, "Take a man by his word and a bull by its horn." Its government ranks first for the least amount of corruption in the world. A strong sense of national pride permeates Finnish identity; Finns are particularly proud of the nation's honorable wartime achievements, world-class athletes, and technological prowess.

LANGUAGE

As of July 2005, Finland's population was estimated to be 5,223,442 people, ranking it 112 in the world, with a population even smaller than that found in New York City. A Finn may speak Finnish, Swedish (just under 6 percent are Swedish-speaking), or Sámi (about 7,000 native speakers). Swedish is the country's second official language, and most Swedish-speaking Finns speak Finnish as well, except along the coastal regions and the Åland Islands where only Swedish is used. Educated Finns and those holding public office are often versed in both Finnish and Swedish, and many public institutions are bilingually named. Television programs are aired in both languages.

The Swedish Theatre in Helsinki

English is also widely used, especially in the business world. French, Spanish, and Russian are taught in schools, and with Finland's admission into the EU, more urgency has been placed on learning those European languages. A small group of older Finns are familiar with German. Strangely, Latin—a "dead" language—is featured weekly on a popular news broadcast by the Finnish Broadcasting Company (YLE).

MANNERS AND CUSTOMS

Finns are known for their reverence of silence. A Finn will rarely engage a stranger in conversation. Tourists may also notice how Finns riding public transportation are unusually silent. In Finnish culture, small talk is considered trivial—even impolite or insincere—and so the typical Finn is lacking in such skills. Finns are not antisocial or unfriendly; they just think before they speak, and speak slowly and with purpose. A Finn means what she says, and expects you do to the same.

The advent of the cellular phone has somewhat changed the world's view of Finns. Nokia, a leading brand of mobile technology, was created in Finland, and the country has since assimilated

A Lutheran chuch in Hanko, Finland

into the wave of cellular communication. Despite their love of silence, Finns are constantly on their mobile phones, and as in in the United States, they download customizable features like ring tones and screensavers. However, mobile phone usage is not allowed in hospitals, and planes, and is considered unacceptable in meetings, concerts, theaters, and church.

Another entirely Finnish custom is **sauna** bathing. There are nearly 1.5 million saunas in Finland. Sauna bathing can take place several times a week and is considered a place to forget about work and release stress. Men and women do not bathe together, unless they are family, and public saunas provide separate facilities for men and women. It is customary to complete an evening with a round in the sauna, followed by conversation and perhaps a light meal.

RELIGION

Religious freedom has been guaranteed in Finland since 1923. Still, 89 percent of Finns belong to the Evangelical-Lutheran Church—a result of Martin Luther's sweeping gains through Eastern Europe during the Reformation. About 1 percent of the country belongs to the Orthodox Church of Finland.

Combined, Baptists, Methodists, Jews, and Muslims comprise another 1 percent of the population. Nine percent of Finns report they do not belong to any religious group. Even though a Finn may not be familiar with a religion different from his own, he is expected to respect other people's personal religious beliefs.

Although most Finns belong to some religious denomination, they do not actively participate in organized church rituals. However, religious holidays like Christmas and Easter, and life events like baptisms, marriages, and funerals, are widely attended and play important roles in Finnish culture.

FOOD

Finnish cuisine mixes European, Scandinavian, and Russian influences. Lighter fare has taken the place of traditional fat-rich dishes, and younger generations of Finns are increasingly health conscious. Healthier vegetable fats have replaced animal fats traditionally found in sausages. Also, Finns have always cooked with nutritious ingredients like rye and other healthful grains.

The biggest family meal is breakfast, which can consist of porridge, bran, cereal, yogurt, milk, and bread. Breakfast can be very hearty and is similar in size to an American lunch. Lunch is somewhat smaller and occurs sometime between 11 A.M. and 1 P.M. Although alcohol is customarily consumed with food, it is rarely served at lunch. Dinner is usually between 6 and 7 P.M.

Traditional dishes are sausages, black pud-

The University of Helsinki

ding with lingonberry sauce, rieska flat breads, and reindeer stew with mashed potatoes. *Kalakukko* fish pie is a loaf-shaped pastry filled with fish and fatty pork. Smoked Baltic herring is popular along the coast. Coffee is more popular than tea and is usually served to end a meal. Finns may also drink water, milk, buttermilk, or beer with their meals. Wine is not as widely enjoyed as it is in other European nations.

EDUCATION

According to the Organisation for Economic Co-operation and Development, Finland's fifteen-year-olds have the best literary skills in the world. They are also top-rated in math and the sciences. This reflects Finland's commitment to provide free public education to its youth. Children begin school at the age of seven and remain enrolled until the age of seventeen. Because Finland is bilingual, both Finnish-speaking and Swedish-speaking schools exist. Some schools use other languages to accommodate immigrant children. Public education includes free lunch, school health care, and transportation to and from school. Very few Finnish children do not attend school.

The school curriculum is similar to that taught in North America. Students study their native language, foreign languages, history, math, the sciences, music, art, physical education, and home economics. Religious instruction may be given in public schools, depending on the denomination of its students. Parents can demand the teaching of a certain religion if a percentage of students belong to that religion.

About half of students continue on to secondary schools. Like Finland's public schools, secondary schools are free to attend and provide lunch without charge. Programs last about three years, at the end of which, students take the national **matriculation** exam. This exam determines whether students can continue their studies at an institution of higher education. Students may also choose to attend vocational schools. These programs also last three years, and give instruction in both general education and job training. Only 6 percent of students choose not to go on to a secondary or vocational school.

Institutions of higher education include polytechnics and universities. Polytechnic centers give vocational instruction at a higher professional level than vocational schools. Universities, similar to those found in North America, are centers for scientific research and the advanced study of conventional academic disciplines. Higher education is also free, but acceptance is competitive; only two-thirds of applicants are admitted into a program of study.

THE ARTS

Finland values freedom of expression, and this attitude has fostered an atmosphere that encourages many artists. Finland's reputation for outstanding art and design was recognized in 2005, and the year was declared "Design Year in Finland." Throughout the year, hundreds of exhibitions, competitions, and forums took place both in the country and around the world, celebrating Finland's artistic achievements.

ARCHITECTURE

In 2001, the World Architecture Award was presented to Rauno Lehtinen, Pekka Maki, and Toni Peltola for their design of the Finnish Embassy in Berlin. Two of the three designers were still working toward their architecture degrees while the embassy was built. The three began their design as part of a competition—a traditional method of introducing new Finnish architects to the industry.

The nation's most widely recognized master architect, Alvar Aalto, was also the winner of one such competition in the 1920s. His work consists of both interior and exterior designs, and demonstrates creative uses of light, curved forms, unusual wood treatments, and a peaceful balance with surrounding natural elements.

Some experts consider Finland the best-designed country in Europe. A sense of order and organization are characteristic of Finnish architecture. Form, content, and background are also important factors in architectural design. The Museum of Finnish Architecture, located in Helsinki, features astounding and historical architectural works.

Famous Finnish Artists
Alvar Aalto, architect
Margareta Capsia, painter
Albert Edelfelt, painter
Akseli Gallen-Kellela, pictorial arts
Renny Harlin, film director
Iittala, glass design
Tove Jansson, children's author
Mika Karuismäki, film director
Aleksis Kivi, author
Marimekko, fashion
Karita Mattila, opera singer
J. L. Runeberg, poet
Matti Salminen, opera singer
Esa-Pekka Salonen, composer
Jukka Pekka Saraste, composer
Jorma Uotinen, dancer and choreographer
Mika Waltari, author

MUSIC

Finland has a long tradition of classical composers, beginning with Erik Tulinberg in the late eighteenth century, who composed several six string quartets. During the 1800s, Helsinki began to cultivate a music culture, and in 1852, the German-born conductor Fredrik Pacius composed the first Finnish opera. Pacius, who immigrated to Finland and also penned the country's national anthem, is called the "father of Finnish music." The Kansanvalistusseura (Society for Culture and Education) was built in 1874 and staged musical events like the Jyvaskula song festival in 1881, which led to the rapid growth in the number of choirs throughout Finland. Events like this helped establish Finland's identity as a land of choirs. The following year would be a momentous time for Finnish music, when the Helsinki University Chorus and the Helsinki Orchestral Society—now known as the Helsinki Philharmonic Orchestra—were formed. Martin Wegelius founded the Helsinki Music Institute, now the Sibelius Academy, that same year.

Jean Sibelius is a leading national figure in Finland's history. His seven symphonies and Violin Concerto are recognized around the world. His works focused on a feeling of national self-esteem and the spirit of country. About the same time

Monument honoring Sibelius in Helsinki

Helsinki's House of Culture

Sibelius's epics were performed in cities, Oskar Merkanto, a writer, conductor, and performer, provided concerts that were musically accessible to people of all classes.

In the following decades, opera would emerge as a powerful aspect of Finnish musical identity. Aarre Merkianto's opera *Juha* is today considered the most important opera in Finnish history. Composed in 1923, *Juha* did not premiere on stage until 1964, because musical contemporaries considered it too difficult to perform. Erik Bergman and Einar Englund were important composers of the 1940s, influenced by innovations in other European styles of opera. The 1950s followed the **Neoclassical** style of composition, and by the 1970s, Finland had become known for its unique brand of music.

CONTEMPORARY ART

Finland has several museums, but in the past few years, the focus of its art world has gravitated toward metropolitan Helsinki. The **postmodernism** movement of the 1980s and some interesting works of the 1990s reflect a sort of self-consciousness. They often convey self-critical themes. New art often uses a collage of techniques and mediums to compose diverse styles; it is a mix of figurative and abstract art. Examples of works in this style are kept in the Kiasma, the new Museum of Contemporary Art in Helsinki.

A child has fun playing in one of Helsinki's fountains

5 THE CITIES

The majority of Finland's population resides in metropolitan areas located in the southern region. Most of the country has fully embraced Finland's status as a technological powerhouse, and its people tend to be savvy in electronics and communication.

Hyperadvanced technologies benefit the various cities by providing efficient solutions to transportation, energy usage, and infrastructure.

HELSINKI

Helsinki was established as the capital of Finland in 1812. It is located on the southern tip of the country surrounded by water on three sides; however, the city was originally founded at the mouth of the Vantaa River in 1550. About 1.2 million people make their home in Helsinki, Finland's most populated city. People in their thirties are the largest group of Helsinki residents.

Helsinki is Finland's largest industrial center, with electronics and shipbuilding businesses located there. This makes Helsinki one of the most **digitized** capitals in the world. Despite technology's strong presence, most jobs in Helsinki are in the public or private **service industries**.

The standard of living in Helsinki is considerably high, and price levels are lower than in other Nordic countries. About 5.4 percent of Helsinki's residents are unemployed, but this number is on the decline. Residents also enjoy a pure and clean-tasting water supply and relatively low air pollution. This is because of efficient water purification and treatment systems and the absence of smokestacks in the industrial sector.

Transportation is well organized in this bustling city; traffic is smooth, and traffic jams are infrequent. Travelers can make a trip across Helsinki in about thirty minutes. Buses, trams, subways, and taxis are also available. Helsinki takes pride in a **synchronized** and punctual public transportation system.

ESPOO

Espoo is Finland's second most populated city. Located northwest of Helsinki, it is considered part of that city's metropolitan area. Espoo is an important city for high-technology education; the Helsinki University of Technology and the Espoo-Vantaa Institute of Technology are located here. Nokia is also based in this city.

Espoo has always made an effort to preserve nature, even during its development. The city is also home to many cultural outlets. The Espoo Cultural Centre hosts international music festivals, like April Jazz and Espoo Ciné, as well as dance and theater events. In addition to showcasing the performing arts, the Centre also has a library.

The Espoo Church, which dates back to medieval years, is constructed of gray granite. Its oldest parts may have been built in the 1480s by an unknown architect today referred to as "Espoo Master." The church is the most important building in the city.

The city of Tampere

TAMPERE

Founded in 1779, Tampere is Finland's third-largest city with a population of about 200,000 people. It is located north of Helsinki in the middle of southern Finland, between the rapids of lakes Näsijärvi and Pyhäjärvi.

Tampere is an important trade center, and has been so since the eleventh century. Today, it is recognized as a leader in textiles in northern Europe.

View of the city of Turku

Other industries important in Tampere include locomotive works, leather, lumber, and machinery.

Tampere is famous for its local specialty, *mustmakkara*, black sausage. The sausage gets its black color from a mixture of pig's blood, rye, and barley. (Tourists report it tastes better than it sounds.) It is traditionally eaten with lingonberry jam and is sold by outdoor vendors and indoor food shops.

TURKU

Deeply rooted in the country's history, Turku is one of Finland's oldest cities. For that reason, it is called the "cradle of Finnish culture." Its fertile agriculture sustained life for early Finnic inhabitants. Turku was the capital of Finland until 1812, when Finland became a Grand Duchy of Russia. The first national university was founded in Turku in 1640, but like the city's status as capital, it too moved to Helsinki in 1827 after a fire wiped out most of the city.

Turku is Finland's largest winter port, located in the southwestern corner of the country. Today, it remains an important center for shipbuilding, machinery, food, textiles, and tourism. Two universities are based there, as well as an art academy. It is the capital of the southwest Finland region and offers many cultural events. The Turku Music Festival and the rock concert Ruisrock are among Scandinavia's oldest festivals. Turku also hosts two seasonal markets: the Medieval Market is held at the end of July, and the Old Time Christmas Market is held before the holiday.

OULU

The city of Oulu takes its name from the Oulu River, where it was founded along the shore of the Gulf of Bothnia in 1605 by the Swedish king Carl IX. Today it is the largest city in northern Finland and is home to the country's second-largest university, Oulu University, founded in 1958. Historically, Oulu is known for products like tar and salmon. Currently, the city provides the most jobs in the region, followed by hospitals, Nokia, and the university. Like other cities in Finland, Oulu has strived to make electronics and Internet technologies a priority in its industrial sector. Other industries like wood refining and paper and steel manufacturing are also strong in Oulu.

In the summer, events like open-air markets occur around Rotuaari Street, located centrally in the city. Oulu, too, has a cultural center, symphony orchestra, music center, theater, and many public museums.

The EU flag

6 THE FORMATION OF THE EUROPEAN UNION

CHAPTER

The EU is an economic and political confederation of twenty-five European nations. Member countries abide by common foreign and security policies and cooperate on judicial and domestic affairs. The confederation, however, does not replace existing states or governments. Each of the twenty-five member states is ***autonomous***, but they have all agreed to establish some common institutions and to hand over some of their own decision-making powers to these international bodies. As a result, decisions on matters that interest all member states can be made democratically, accommodating everyone's concerns and interests.

Today, the EU is the most powerful regional organization in the world. It has evolved from a primarily economic organization to an increasingly political one. Besides promoting economic cooperation, the EU requires that its members uphold fundamental values of peace and **solidarity**, human dignity, freedom, and equality. Based on the principles of democracy and the rule of law, the EU respects the culture and organizations of member states.

HISTORY

The seeds of the EU were planted more than fifty years ago in a Europe reduced to smoking piles of rubble by two world wars. European nations suffered great financial difficulties in the postwar period. They were struggling to get back on their feet and realized that another war would cause further hardship. Knowing that internal conflict was hurting all of Europe, a drive began toward European cooperation.

France took the first historic step. On May 9, 1950 (now celebrated as Europe Day), Robert Schuman, the French foreign minister, proposed the coal and steel industries of France and West Germany be coordinated under a single supranational authority. The proposal, known as the Treaty

of Paris, attracted four other countries—Belgium, Luxembourg, the Netherlands, and Italy—and resulted in the 1951 formation of the European Coal and Steel Community (ECSC). These six countries became the founding members of the EU.

In 1957, European cooperation took its next big leap. Under the Treaty of Rome, the European Economic Community (EEC) and the European Atomic Energy Community (EURATOM) were formed. Informally known as the Common Market, the EEC promoted joining the national economies into a single European economy. The 1965 Treaty of Brussels (more commonly referred to as the Merger Treaty) united these various treaty organizations under a single umbrella, the European Community (EC).

In 1992, the Maastricht Treaty (also known as the Treaty of the European Union) was signed in Maastricht, the Netherlands, signaling the birth of the EU as it stands today. **Ratified** the following year, the Maastricht Treaty provided for a central banking system, a common currency (the euro) to replace the national currencies, a legal definition of the EU, and a framework for expanding the

The EU's united economy has allowed it to become a worldwide financial power.

EU's political role, particularly in the area of foreign and security policy.

By 1993, the member countries completed their move toward a single market and agreed to participate in a larger common market, the European Economic Area, established in 1994.

The EU, headquartered in Brussels, Belgium, reached its current member strength in spurts. In

1973, Denmark, Ireland, and the United Kingdom joined the six founding members of the EC. They were followed by Greece in 1981, and Portugal and Spain in 1986. The 1990s saw the unification of the two Germanys, and as a result, East Germany entered the EU fold. Austria, Finland, and Sweden joined the EU in 1995, bringing the total number of member states to fifteen. In 2004, the EU nearly doubled its size when ten countries—Cyprus, the Czech Republic, Estonia, Hungary, Latvia, Lithuania, Malta, Poland, Slovakia, and Slovenia—became members.

THE EU FRAMEWORK

The EU's structure has often been compared to a "roof of a temple with three columns." As established by the Maastricht Treaty, this three-pillar framework encompasses all the policy areas—or pillars—of European cooperation. The three pillars of the EU are the European Community, the Common Foreign and Security Policy (CFSP), and Police and Judicial Co-operation in Criminal Matters.

QUICK FACTS: THE EUROPEAN UNION

Number of Member Countries: 25
Official Languages: 20—Czech, Danish, Dutch, English, Estonian, Finnish, French, German, Greek, Hungarian, Italian, Latvian, Lithuanian, Maltese, Polish, Portuguese, Slovak, Slovenian, Spanish, and Swedish; additional language for treaty purposes: Irish Gaelic
Motto: *In Varietate Concordia* (United in Diversity)
European Council's President: Each member state takes a turn to lead the council's activities for 6 months.
European Commission's President: José Manuel Barroso (Portugal)
European Parliament's President: Josep Borrell (Spain)
Total Area: 1,502,966 square miles (3,892,685 sq. km.)
Population: 454,900,000
Population Density: 302.7 people/square mile (116.8 people/sq. km.)
GDP: €9.61.1012
Per Capita GDP: €21,125
Formation:
- Declared: February 7, 1992, with signing of the Maastricht Treaty
- Recognized: November 1, 1993, with the ratification of the Maastricht Treaty

Community Currency: Euro. Currently 12 of the 25 member states have adopted the euro as their currency.
Anthem: "Ode to Joy"
Flag: Blue background with 12 gold stars arranged in a circle
Official Day: Europe Day, May 9

Source: europa.eu.int

PILLAR ONE

The European Community pillar deals with economic, social, and environmental policies. It is a body consisting of the European Parliament, European Commission, European Court of Justice, Council of the European Union, and the European Courts of Auditors.

PILLAR TWO

The idea that the EU should speak with one voice in world affairs is as old as the European integration process itself. Toward this end, the Common Foreign and Security Policy (CFSP) was formed in 1993.

PILLAR THREE

The cooperation of EU member states in judicial and criminal matters ensures that its citizens enjoy the freedom to travel, work, and live securely and safely anywhere within the EU. The third pillar—Police and Judicial Co-operation in Criminal Matters—helps to protect EU citizens from international crime and to ensure equal access to justice and fundamental rights across the EU.

The flags of the EU's nations:

top row, left to right
Belgium, the Czech Republic, Denmark, Germany, Estonia, Greece

second row, left to right
Spain, France, Ireland, Italy, Cyprus, Latvia

third row, left to right
Lithuania, Luxembourg, Hungary, Malta, the Netherlands, Austria

bottom row, left to right
Poland, Portugal, Slovenia, Slovakia, Finland, Sweden, United Kingdom

ECONOMIC STATUS

As of May 2004, the EU had the largest economy in the world, followed closely by the United States. But even though the EU continues to enjoy a trade surplus, it faces the twin problems of high unemployment rates and ***stagnancy***.

The 2004 addition of ten new member states is expected to boost economic growth. EU membership is likely to stimulate the economies of these relatively poor countries. In turn, their prosperity growth will be beneficial to the EU.

THE EURO

The EU's official currency is the euro, which came into circulation on January 1, 2002. The shift to the euro has been the largest monetary changeover in the world. Twelve countries—Belgium, Germany, Greece, Spain, France, Ireland, Italy, Luxembourg, the Netherlands, Finland, Portugal, and Austria—have adopted it as their currency.

SINGLE MARKET

Within the EU, laws of member states are harmonized and domestic policies are coordinated to create a larger, more-efficient single market.

The chief features of the EU's internal policy on the single market are:

- free trade of goods and services

- a common EU competition law that controls anticompetitive activities of companies and member states

- removal of internal border control and harmonization of external controls between member states

- freedom for citizens to live and work anywhere in the EU as long as they are not dependent on the state

- free movement of **capital** between member states

- harmonization of government regulations, corporation law, and trademark registration

- a single currency

- coordination of environmental policy

- a common agricultural policy and a common fisheries policy

- a common system of indirect taxation, the value-added tax (VAT), and common customs duties and **excise**

- funding for research

- funding for aid to disadvantaged regions

The EU's external policy on the single market specifies:

- a common external **tariff** and a common position in international trade negotiations

- funding of programs in other Eastern European countries and developing countries

COOPERATION AREAS

EU member states cooperate in other areas as well. Member states can vote in European Parliament elections. Intelligence sharing and cooperation in criminal matters are carried out through EUROPOL and the Schengen Information System.

The EU is working to develop common foreign and security policies. Many member states are resisting such a move, however, saying these are sensitive areas best left to individual member states. Arguing in favor of a common approach to security and foreign policy are countries like France and Germany, who insist that a safer and more secure Europe can only become a reality under the EU umbrella.

One of the EU's great achievements has been to create a boundary-free area within which people, goods, services, and money can move around freely; this ease of movement is sometimes called "the four freedoms." As the EU grows in size, so do the challenges facing it—and yet its fifty-year history has amply demonstrated the power of cooperation.

The EU believes that it can use its power to act as a "lighthouse" for the rest of the world.

KEY EU INSTITUTIONS

Five key institutions play a specific role in the EU.

THE EUROPEAN PARLIAMENT

The European Parliament (EP) is the democratic voice of the people of Europe. Directly elected every five years, the Members of the European Parliament (MEPs) sit not in national **blocs** but in political groups representing the seven main political parties of the member states. Each group reflects the political ideology of the national parties to which its members belong. Some MEPs are not attached to any political group.

COUNCIL OF THE EUROPEAN UNION

The Council of the European Union (formerly known as the Council of Ministers) is the main leg-

EUROPEAN UNION—FINLAND

islative and decision-making body in the EU. It brings together the nationally elected representatives of the member-state governments. One minister from each of the EU's member states attends council meetings. It is the forum in which government representatives can assert their interests and reach compromises. Increasingly, the Council of the European Union and the EP are acting together as colegislators in decision-making processes.

EUROPEAN COMMISSION

The European Commission does much of the day-to-day work of the EU. Politically independent, the commission represents the interests of the EU as a whole, rather than those of individual member states. It drafts proposals for new European laws, which it presents to the EP and the Council of the European Union. The European ...sion makes sure EU decisions are imple- properly and supervises the way EU re spent. It also sees that everyone abides European treaties and European law. EU member-state governments choose the an Commission president, who is then ...d by the EP. Member states, in consulta- ...h the incoming president, nominate the ...ropean Commission members, who must approved by the EP. The commission is

appointed for a five-year term, but can be dismissed by the EP. Many members of its staff work in Brussels, Belgium.

COURT OF JUSTICE

Headquartered in Luxembourg, the Court of Justice of the European Communities consists of one independent judge from each EU country. This court ensures that the common rules decided in the EU are understood and followed uniformly by all the members. The Court of Justice settles disputes over how EU treaties and legislation are interpreted. If national courts are in doubt about how to apply EU rules, they must ask the Court of Justice. Individuals can also bring proceedings against EU institutions before the court.

COURT OF AUDITORS

EU funds must be used legally, economically, and for their intended purpose. The Court of Auditors, an independent EU institution located in Luxembourg, is responsible for overseeing how EU money is spent. In effect, these auditors help European taxpayers get better value for the money that has been channeled into the EU.

OTHER IMPORTANT BODIES

1. European Economic and Social Committee: expresses the opinions of organized civil society on economic and social issues

2. Committee of the Regions: expresses the opinions of regional and local authorities

3. European Central Bank: responsible for monetary policy and managing the euro

4. European Ombudsman: deals with citizens' complaints about mismanagement by any EU institution or body

5. European Investment Bank: helps achieve EU objectives by financing investment projects

Together with a number of agencies and other bodies completing the system, the EU's institutions have made it the most powerful organization in the world.

EU MEMBER STATES

In order to become a member of the EU, a country must have a stable democracy that guarantees the rule of law, human rights, and protection of minorities. It must also have a functioning market economy as well as a civil service capable of applying and managing EU laws.

The EU provides substantial financial assistance and advice to help candidate countries prepare themselves for membership. As of October 2004, the EU has twenty-five member states. Bulgaria and Romania are likely to join in 2007, which would bring the EU's total population to nearly 500 million.

In December 2004, the EU decided to open negotiations with Turkey on its proposed membership. Turkey's possible entry into the EU has been fraught with controversy. Much of this controversy has centered on Turkey's human rights record and the divided island of Cyprus. If allowed to join the EU, Turkey would be its most-populous member state.

The 2004 expansion was the EU's most ambitious enlargement to date. Never before has the EU embraced so many new countries, grown so much in terms of area and population, or encompassed so many different histories and cultures. As the EU moves forward into the twenty-first century, it will undoubtedly continue to grow in both political and economic strength.

Competition in the Tammerkoski River in Tampere

CHAPTER 7 FINLAND IN THE EUROPEAN UNION

Finland became a member of the EU on January 1, 1995, following a referendum posed to citizens in October of 1994 that yielded 57 percent of the vote in favor of joining. By November, parliament had approved membership in the EU by a vote of 152 to 45, and within a couple months, Finland was inducted alongside Austria and Sweden. In 2002, Finland fully adopted the euro as its national currency.

Since joining, the country has received considerable assistance from Brussels. Finland—and particularly its capital, Helsinki—has expanded its focus to the whole of Europe, and also to improving relations with other Nordic countries, Russia, and the Baltic states of the former USSR. It has pushed for the incorporation of these and other central and eastern European countries into the EU, in order to strengthen their economic ties and to increase national security. In terms of the formation of a common foreign and security policy for all EU member states, Finland supports intergovernmentalism—a system that favors the independent will of each individual nation over an overall organizational policy. This is because Finland wishes to reserve the right to remain neutral in times of conflict. An all-encompassing EU foreign policy may require Finland to become militarily aligned with other member states during war times.

Sunrise over one of Finland's many lakes

FINLAND AS PRESIDENT

From July to December of 1999, Finland assumed the EU presidency. Many consider it to have been a productive time, with many goals accomplished that were outlined at the beginning of the term. At the Helsinki Summit, a clear plan was established to increase the number of EU member states. Also, during a meeting of the European Council in Tampere, guidelines were set for handling cases of international crime and cross-border security.

THE PROS AND PITFALLS OF EU MEMBERSHIP

A survey conducted by the Finnish Ministry of Foreign Affairs in early 2000 revealed that Finns felt membership in the EU brought advantages to wage and salary workers but not to farmers, and has helped increase Finns' knowledge about other European nations. However, a large portion of people polled expected **bureaucracy** to increase in coming years.

One effect of EU membership was the lifting of import restrictions on alcoholic beverages. For several decades, Finland's government maintained a **monopoly** over the retail sale of alcohol and taxed imported liquors heavily. Today, Finns can purchase alcohol in other nations at a cost of about 50 percent less than what they pay domestically. The problem with this, however, is that when abused, alcohol can become an addictive and dangerous substance. About 2,500 people die of alcohol abuse in Finland every year, and about 26,000 violent crimes in Finland involve alcohol. Whether the availability of cheaper alcohol has any long-term effects on these statistics is yet to be known.

Another change in taxation came in 2002. For many years, the price of a new car in Finland could include as much as 50 percent sales tax. Also, cars bought outside the country were subject to steep vehicle taxation imposed by Finnish customs. The European Court of Justice in Luxemburg took up the issue in September of 2002. As a result, Finland made huge cuts to automobile taxes. Around the country, the price of new and used cars dropped dramatically.

One obvious disadvantage of EU membership was felt by Finnish agriculture. Immediately after accession, produce dropped to half its previous price. Suddenly, farmers were responsible for making up this lost percentage of profit. Also, as predicted by the 2000 survey, the amount of paperwork involved in filing for government aid increased tremendously; frustrated, many farmers simply gave up farming. The number of active farms dropped by about 25,000 during Finland's formative years of EU membership.

FINLAND'S FUTURE IN THE EU

Finland's reputation as an exemplary member nation shows that a small nation can still have a big impact when it comes to politics on the world stage. Finland continues to work cooperatively with other nations to increase membership in the EU, and to improve political, economic, and social relations throughout the world.

A Calendar of Finnish Festivals

Finland celebrates many holidays and festivals. Some of these events originated from the time when seasonal changes dictated the rhythm of life for Finnish farmers. Finns also honor national personalities and achievements with their own public holidays.

January: January 1 is New Year's Day. To celebrate, Finns pour melted tin into cold water to cast irregular shapes. The shadows cast by these strange sculptures are said to reveal information about the future. Fireworks, champagne, and buffet feasts all play a part in the celebration. January 6 is **Epiphany**, or the christening of Jesus. Orthodox churches in Finland sanctify water in observance of this holiday.

February: February 5 is **J. L. Runeberg's Day**. J. L. Runeberg was a Finnish poet who achieved world fame. Finns commemorate his life by eating "Runeberg's tarts," moist pastries with icing and raspberry jam. **Friendship Day** falls on February 14. It is similar to Valentine's Day in North America. Schoolchildren make and send cards on this day, while various organizations promote health education and charity. **Kalevala's Day** celebrates the publication of *The Kalevala*, the first national epic in Finland.

March: The week before Easter, on **Palm Sunday**, children dress up like Easter witches and go door-to-door carrying sprigs of willow. They are often rewarded with sweets or money, much like Halloween in North American countries. **Good Friday** takes place on the Friday before **Easter Sunday**. Easter traditions include children growing grass on plates indoors, decorating Easter eggs, and making Easter cards. Finns will dine on lamb, breads, and pudding served with cream and sprinkled sugar.

April: April Fools' Day lands on the first day of the month. Finns play jokes on one another, and newspapers, television, and radio shows may broadcast fictitious stories. Finns also recite the poem, "April fool, April fool, eat some herring and drink muddy water on top of it all!" On April 9, Finns commemorate the life of Michael Agricola with **Michael Agricola's Day**. He is regarded as the first developer of the Finnish written language.

May: May 1 is **May Day**, or *Vappu*, the celebration of spring. Street carnivals and drinking festivities will take place even if it is still snowing. Music, singing, and bonfires mark the eve of May Day, or **Walpurgis Night**. **Mothers' Day** falls on the second Sunday of the month. The official flag is raised on this day, and mothers receive cards and flowers from their children. Ascension Day takes place forty days after Easter, and shops are closed on this day. **Whitsunday** takes place fifty days after Easter. Christians regard this day as the birth of the church.

June: In the third week of June, during the summer solstice, come **Midsummer Eve** and **Midsummer Day**. This is a time to celebrate nature and the countryside. Many Finns celebrate the polar days by lighting *kokko*, or bonfires, at their summer cottage, or by decorating their urban homes with birch branches or lilacs. In Swedish-speaking areas along the coast of Finland, maypoles are put up to celebrate the holiday.

July: July 6 is **Eino Leino's Day**. Eino Leino was a Finnish poet and novelist who lived during the early twentieth century. His greatest works were inspired by *The Kalevala*.

October: October 10 is **Aleksis Kivi's Day**. Kivi is regarded as the creator of modern Finnish literature. In 1870, he wrote the classic Finnish novel *The Seven Brothers*, which achieved world fame. **United Nation's Day** falls on October 24, and commemorates the day when the organization was founded.

November: the first Saturday of November is **All Saints Day**, a silent and thoughtful occasion when families bring flowers and candles to the graves of their loved ones, and attend church services. **Fathers' Day** arrives on November 13. Fathers are served breakfast in bed and receive small cards and gifts from their families.

December: December 6 is **Independence Day**. It commemorates the day Finland officially declared its independence from Russia and became its own country for the first time. Finns light candles in their windows on this day to honor the historic event. The main feast holiday of Finland also arrives in December—**Christmas**. The main Christmas meal is held on **Christmas Eve**, on December 24. At midday on Christmas Eve, "Christmas Peace" is declared across the country, a ceremonial opening of the Christmas season. At dusk, families light candles at the graves of their loved ones. Later, Father Christmas delivers gifts to each family. On Christmas Day, families attend church services, or children's plays, and may engage in charity or other family traditions.

The day after Christmas is **Boxing Day**. Boxing day is a holiday of charity. Organizations take up collections, and instead of sending Christmas cards, offices will donate money to charities in the name of their employees.

Meatballs (Lihapullat)

Serves 4–5 people

Ingredients
7 oz. minced beef
1/2 cup fine dry breadcrumbs or two slices of
white bread
1/2 cup cream
1 onion
1 tablespoon oil
1 egg
1 teaspoon salt
1/4 teaspoon allspice or white pepper

Gravy:
2 tablespoons fat
2 tablespoons flour
2 cups pan juices

Directions
Mix breadcrumbs with water and cream in a
bowl. Let stand until the breadcrumbs are
absorbed. Finely chop the onion and sauté in
oil in a frying pan or microwave oven. Add the
onion, egg, seasonings, and meat. Mix until
smooth. Wet your hands and shape the mixture
into balls. Fry meatballs on all sides in hot fat.
Small balls will be done in 3–5 minutes, larger
ones 5–8 minutes.

To make gravy, brown the flour lightly in fat.
Add the liquid, stirring all the time. Add the
cream and check seasonings. The gravy can be
served separately or poured over the meatballs.
Serve with potatoes and grated carrots.

Lingonberry jam and gherkins also go well with
the dish.

May Day Cookies (*Tippaleivät*)

Ingredients
2 eggs
2 teaspoons sugar
1 teaspoon salt
1 cup milk
2 cups flour
1/2 teaspoon vanilla
vegetable or coconut oil for frying

Directions
Mix the eggs and sugar, but don't beat! Add
the other ingredients and stir into a smooth batter.

Put the batter into a paper cone or a pastry
bag fitted with a small-holed nozzle. Squeeze
the batter in a thin band into the hot oil. Use a
spiral motion to form nest-like cookies. If possible, use a metal ring in the pot to keep the
cookies in shape.

When the cookies have turned golden
brown, remove and drain them on paper tow-
els. Dust the cold cookies with powdered sugar.

Pancakes (*Ohukaiset*)

Ingredients
2 1/2 cups milk or 1 1/4 cup cream and 1
1/4 cups water

3/4 cup flour
2 eggs
1 teaspoon salt

Mix the flour and the milk. Add the salt and beat in the eggs. Let the batter stand for a minute before frying. Fry pancakes on a hot pan, greased with butter or margarine. Serve with sweet jam.

To make a sheet pancake from the same batter, pour into a greased baking pan or frying pan and bake in the oven at 425°F (approximately 220°C) until golden brown.

Runeberg's Tart

Makes 8 tarts

Ingredients
1 egg
1 1/2 tablespoons sugar
3 tablespoons brown sugar
1 teaspoon vanilla sugar
1/2 cup butter
3 tablespoons cream
3/4 cup flour
1 teaspoon baking powder
1/4 cup ground almonds

Syrup:
1/2 cup water
1/2 cup fruit punch
2 tablespoons sugar

Topping:
thick raspberry jam
powdered sugar
1 teaspoon water

Directions
Cream together the softened butter and sugars. In another bowl and with clean beaters, whip the cream until it's light. Add the egg and whipped cream into the butter-sugar foam. Mix together dry ingredients and fold them lightly into the batter. Slightly butter 8 small cylindrical moulds and fill them with batter. (You can also use cupcake tins.) Place moulds on a baking sheet and bake at 400°F (approximately 200°C) for 20–30 minutes.

In a medium saucepan, combine the water, punch, and sugar and bring to a boil. When the tarts are ready, drizzle them with warm syrup. Let them absorb the syrup for at least an hour. Remove tarts gently from the moulds. Cut out a little piece from the tops, if the tarts aren't even. With a spoon, make little holes on the top of the tarts and fill them with raspberry jam. Let the tarts set in the fridge.

Combine the powdered sugar and 1 teaspoon of water to make the icing. Put the icing into a paper cone or a pastry bag fitted with a small-holed nozzle. Squeeze the icing onto the tarts, forming a ring around the raspberry jam. Let the icing set and serve tarts with coffee or tea.

PROJECT AND REPORT IDEAS

Maps

- Create a map of Finland. Use different colored markers or crayons to highlight the areas that once belonged to Russia.
- Create a map of Finland illustrating the different geographic regions of the country.

Reports

- Write a brief report on Finland's technology industry.
- Write a report on Finland's role within the EU.
- Finland has many famous artists, architects, dancers, musicians, and writers. Many of them are listed in chapter 4. Select one of these people from the list, or research another one on your own, and write a brief report about their work and success.

Journal

- Imagine you are a student in Finland as the country falls into famine and war during the late 1800s. Write a journal entry discussing your feelings about the great struggles your country is facing.
- Imagine you are taking a trip to Finland. Create an itinerary of the historical sites, museums, and galleries you would like to visit and why.

Projects

- Learn the Finnish or Swedish expressions for simple words such as hello, good day, please, and thank you. Try them on your friends.
- Make a calendar of your country's festivals and list the ones that are common or similar in Finland. Are they celebrated differently in Finland? If so, how?
- Go online or to the library and find images of an important Finnish building. Create a model of it.
- Make a poster advertising a tourist destination in Finland.
- Make a list of all the rivers, places, seas, and islands that you have read about in this book and indicate them on a map of Finland.

- Find a Finnish recipe other than the ones given in this book, and ask an adult to help you make it. Share it with members of your class.

Group Activities

- Debate: One side should take the role of Sweden and the other Russia. Both sides should discuss why they deserve control of Finland.
- Research a Finnish play. Perform one of its scenes for your class.

CHRONOLOGY

10000 BCE	The first human settlement is established in Finland.
8000 BCE	Neolithic peoples settle in Finland.
3000 BCE	The pottery-making culture arrives in Finland.
1800–1600 BCE	Battle-Axe culture brings agriculture to Finland.
1600–1200 BCE	Finland experiences its Iron Age.
500 CE	Vikings use the area of Finland to build merchant posts to trade with Russia and the Middle East.
1323	The Peace of Pahkinasaari establishes a political border between Finland and Russia.
1150s	King Erik and Bishop Henry lead a crusade to Finland.
1362	Finns granted the right to send representative to vote in Swedish elections.
1543	The first Finnish-language book is printed.
1598	The Lutheran Reformation is adopted in Sweden-Finland.
1617	Sweden becomes the supreme rule of the Baltic Sea with control of the Gulf of Finland.
1640	Abo Academy is the first university founded in Finland.
1741	The Finnish upper class, the Hats, lead a revolution against Russia to regain ceded territories.
1807	An alliance of Russia and France invades Finland.
1809	Sweden formally cedes control of Finland to Russia.
1812	The capital city is moved from Turku to Helsinki.
1835	*The Kalevala* is published.
1860	Finland acquires its own currency, the markka.
1892	Finnish is adopted as the country's second official language.
1917	Finland declares independence from Russia.
1919	A new Finnish constitution is drafted.
1923	Freedom of religion is guaranteed in Finland.
1940	The Winter War ends with Finland ceding strategic territories to the Soviet Union.
1944	Finland signs an armistice with the Soviet Union, agreeing to surrender land and pay reparations.
1947	The Treaty of Paris limits the size of Finland's military.
1952	Finland completes payment of reparations to the Soviets.
1956	Finland regains the land lost to the Soviet Union during World War II.
1955	Finland joins the UN and the Nordic Council.
1961	Finland joins the EFTA.
1969	The Central Organization of the Finnish Trade Unions is formed.
1975	The Helsinki Accords are signed.
1989	Finland joins the Council of Europe.
1995	Finland becomes a member of the EU.
1999	Finland assumes the EU presidency for a six-month term.
2000	A new Finnish constitution takes effect.
2002	Finland places the euro into circulation.
2005	"Design Year in Finland" is declared.

FURTHER READING/INTERNET RESOURCES

Hutchison, Linda. *Finland*. San Diego, Calif.: Lucent Books, 2004.
Kent, Neil. *Helsinki: A Cultural and Literary History*. Northampton, Mass.: Interlink Publishing Group, Inc., 2004.
Leney, Terttu. *Culture Smart! Finland*. Portland, Ore.: Graphic Arts Center Publishing Company, 2004.
Lewis, Richard D. *Finland, Cultural Lone Wolf*. Yarmouth, Maine: Intercultural Press, 2004.
Singleton, Fred. *A Short History of Finland*. Cambridge, U.K.: Cambridge University Press, 2002.

Travel Information
www.lonelyplanet.com/destinations/europe/finland/
www.travel.fi/int/

History and Geography
uk.encarta.msn.com/text_761578960___2/Finland.html
www.infoplease.com

Culture and Festivals
virtual.finland.fi/
www.finnguide.fi/calendar/

Economic and Political Information
www.cia.gov/cia/publications/factbook/
countrystudies.us/finland/110.htm

EU Information
europa.eu.int/

FOR MORE INFORMATION

Embassy of Finland, Washington DC
3301 Massachusetts Avenue NW
Washington DC 20008
Tel.: 202-298-5800
Fax: 202–298-6030
www.finland.org/en

Embassy of the United States in Helsinki
Itäinen Puistotie 14 B
00140 Helsinki. Finland
Tel.: +358-9-616-250

Ministry for Foreign Affairs of Finland
Merikasarmi
P.O. Box 176
00161 Helsinki, Finland
Tel.: +358-9-160-05

European Union
Delegation of the European Commission to the United States
2300 M Street, NW
Washington DC 20037
Tel.: 202-862-9500
Fax: 202-429-1766

GLOSSARY

adversarial: At odds with another party; conflicting.

Allies: During World War II, the alliance formed by Great Britain, France, the Soviet Union, and the United States, to combat the Axis powers of Germany, Italy, and Japan.

antiquated: Old or outdated.

archipelago: A group of islands.

Arctic Circle: A line of latitude near the southern tip of the North Pole.

arctic scrub: A species of plant native to arctic climates.

armistice: A truce, or pact to temporarily stop fighting.

assimilated: Absorbed or incorporated into the prevailing culture.

autocratic: Ruled with absolute authority.

autonomous: Self-governing.

blocs: Groups of countries with shared aims.

bureaucracy: A system of administration that is divided into several departments and that typically operates using inefficient or complex procedures.

cabinet: A leader's group of advisers.

capital: Wealth in the form of money or property.

ceded: Gave control over to another country.

checks and balances: A system in which the powers of each branch of government can limit the powers of the other branches, so that no one branch exercises an unbalanced measure of control.

coniferous-mixed: Cone-bearing trees of various types.

coveted: Wanted very much.

Crusades: Military expeditions made by European Christians in the eleventh and thirteenth centuries to recapture areas taken by Muslim forces.

customs system: The method of collecting taxes on imports.

Diet: Finnish house of government.

digitized: Converted to digital form.

epic: A long narrative poem.

estranging: Making unfriendly.

excise: A government-imposed tax on domestic goods.

fascist: Someone who supports fascism, a system of government characterized by dictatorship, centralized control of private enterprise, repression of all opposition, and extreme nationalism.

Finnicization: To make Finnish in character or quality; to give the characteristic of being from Finland.

Great Depression: A worldwide period of economic decline in the 1930s.

gross domestic product (GDP): The total market value of all the goods and services produced by a nation during a specified period.

hierarchal: Formally ranked.

indigenous: Originating and living or occurring naturally in an area or environment.

infrastructure: A country's large-scale public systems, services, and facilities that are necessary for economic activity.

matriculation: The act of admitting someone as a student.

medieval: Pertaining to the Middle Ages.

monopoly: Having exclusive control over the production or sale of a certain product or service.

nationalism: A strong sense of pride in or devotion to one's country.

Neoclassical: An art and architectural movement of the eighteenth and nineteenth centuries that saw a return to the simple styles of ancient Greece and Rome.

Neolithic: From the cultural period of the Stone Age beginning around 10,000 BCE, characterized by the development of agriculture and the making of stone tools.

parliament: Body of government.

per capita: For each.

perforated: Having holes, especially a row of small holes.

pillage: To rob a place using force, especially during war.

plateau: A raised area with a flat top.

popular vote: Selected by the people in general, not by a select group.

postmodernism: An art, literature, and philosophical movement developed as a reaction to modernism and that saw a return to more traditional elements.

preemptive: Designed to prevent an anticipated situation or occurrence; cautionary.

proximity: Nearness to.

ratified: Officially approved.

reparations: Compensation paid by the loser of a war.

republic: A form of government in which people elect representatives to exercise power for them.

right-wing: The conservative membership of a group.

Russification: To make Russian in character or quality; to give the characteristic of being from Russia.

sauna: A steam bath that results from pouring water over hot rocks.

service industries: Businesses that sell services rather than products.

solidarity: The act of standing together, presenting a united front.

stagnancy: A period of inactivity.

synchronized: operating at precisely the same time.

tariff: Tax levied by governments on goods, usually imports.

theses: Propositions advanced as arguments.

unicameral: One level of organization.

universal suffrage: The right to vote by all citizens of a country.

urbanization: The act of making an area into a town.

INDEX

PICTURE CREDITS

BIOGRAPHIES

AUTHOR

Nicole Sia graduated from Binghamton University in 2004 with a degree in English and rhetoric, and has worked for newspapers, and as a freelance writer and editor. She enjoys learning and writing about different cultures and countries. Her other interests include music, food, art, and pop culture.

SERIES CONSULTANT

Ambassador John Bruton served as Irish Prime Minister from 1994 until 1997. As prime minister, he helped turn Ireland's economy into one of the fastest-growing in the world. He was also involved in the Northern Ireland Peace Process, which led to the 1998 Good Friday Agreement. During his tenure as Ireland's prime minister, he also presided over the European Union presidency in 1996 and helped finalize the Stability and Growth Pact, which governs management of the euro. Before being named the European Commission Head of Delegation in the United States, he was a member of the convention that drafted the European Constitution, signed October 29, 2004.

The European Commission Delegation to the United States represents the interests of the European Union as a whole, much as ambassadors represent their countries' interests to the U.S. government. Matters coming under European Commission authority are negotiated between the commission and the U.S. administration.